Boo's Beard

For Boo, Delilah, Jessie, and all of my future furry friends.

—R. M.

Boo's Beard

Written by
ROSE MANNERING

Illustrated by
BETHANY STRAKER

Sky Pony Press
NEW YORK

Every day, Tom took his dog, Boo, to the park outside his house.

Tom threw sticks for Boo while the other children played on the swings. They didn't play with Tom, because he didn't understand them and they didn't understand him.

Luckily, he had Boo, and Boo was easy to understand.

She wagged her tail when she was happy...

and she whined when she was sad.

Tom loved Boo, but he wished that they could play with the other children, too.

One day, Boo was snuffling in the bushes when a little girl named Lydia stopped to watch.

"That dog is smiling!"
cried Lydia, and the others
came over to look.

They all laughed, but Tom didn't understand.

Lydia twirled Boo's beard up at the ends into an even bigger smile.

"Look! This **smile** means she's **happy**," Lydia told Tom.

Then Lydia changed Boo's beard again.
"This **frown** means she's **sad**," Lydia said.

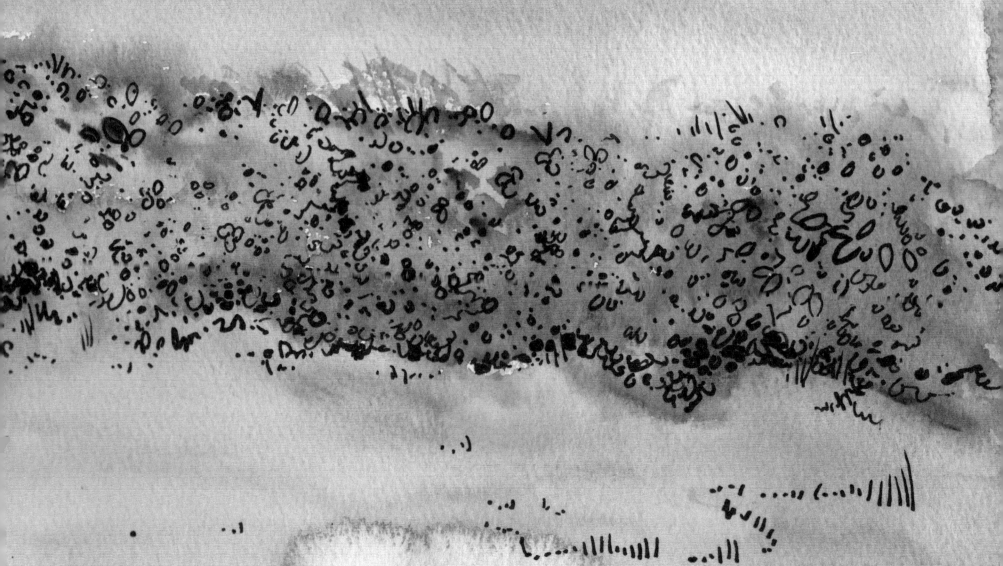

"This means she's **angry!**" said Lydia, fluffing out Boo's beard.

"Come and play with us," said Lydia. "And bring Boo, too."

"Okay," said Tom.
He pointed to his **smile** and said,

"This means I'm **happy**."

Sky Pony Press books may be purchased in bulk at special discounts for sales promotion, corporate gifts, fund-raising, or educational purposes. Special editions can also be created to speci cations. For details, contact the Special Sales Department, Sky Pony Press, 307 West 36th Street, 11th Floor, New York, NY 10018 or info@skyhorsepublishing.com.

Sky Pony® is a registered trademark of Skyhorse Publishing, Inc.®, a Delaware corporation.

Visit our website at www.skyponypress.com.

10 9 8 7 6 5 4 3 2 1

Manufactured in China, June 2015
This product conforms to CPSIA 2008

Library of Congress Cataloging-in-Publication Data is available on file.

Cover design by Sarah Brody
Cover illustration credit Bethany Straker

Print ISBN: 978-1-63450-207-8
Ebook ISBN: 978-1-63450-918-3